TREASURE ISLAND IN OLD MAKEN

BHANUPRIYA RANA

ISBN 979-888606460-5

The story is written in collaboration with people who have worked really hard for publishing this story.

I hope you will like this because being an Author is difficult but accepting many things is really hard.

THIS BOOK IS ALSO WRITTEN IN WAIT OF THE UPCOMING BOOK:

LOVER'S LOVE......

Contents

Foreword

Writing this book, I don't think she is my inspiration but she is the person who forced me to take out all my talent and use it somewhere so I can be confident about it. As the result today she is proud of me and makes me feel like I deserve to be loved or been proud by someone.

The teacher who was behind my success was MS.Niyati Lodha

&

My parents and my friends were always beside me in my dream. One of my best friends and I were together with this dream but we weren't having the same destiny and we fell apart. Since that she focused on her dad's dream and I own her and my to make her one day prod that I made her dream true.

Preface

I am Bhanupriya. I was born in 2008 on 25th April and right now I am 13yrs writing my first book.

I am writing this book for my talent so that it gets expressed to the ones who do even know it.

&

THE first book is a kind of horror as making an audience is the hardest work I have seen but I tried my best to show this up...I hope you would like this.

Preface

Acknowledgements

This book is written with collaboration of:

Mr.Gram

Sabethook

DarkAlliGator

KMApok

CHAPTER - 1- The Kid

Characters are:

JESSIE

JESSIE'S FATHER

JESSIE'S MOTHER

THE PARANORMALIST

THE PRIEST [FATHER]

CHAPTER -2- The Old Maken

Characters are:

MARIA

LIU

MARIA'S BOYFRIEND

CHARLIE [MARIA'S LITTLE BROTHER]

MARIA'S DAUGHTER

THE MINY BOY

ONE

THE KID

Hello, I am Jessie. I am 13yrs and I study in 8th standard. Today I am going to share an incident with all of you. I don't think that you will believe in me but I hear from a paranormalist. I think you will believe me. So, when I was in the last year of 7th standard, This incident happened that time. I was usually on my regular time which was playing games till 2 A.M on my laptop. I hope you all might be thinking at this time I am playing games as the game which I play is online at that till. let's move on to afterward what happened, I was playing my favorite game but suddenly an E-mail appeared with the name LOLIPOP.it is a little weird but that was the name of a gaming E-MAIL is LOLIPOP. I just opened it and read the information, when i read it I get to know that a gaming company is wanted me to apply as I was just 12yrs not apply they mean to become a gamer there, I accepted the form and started playing the game but because of my exams I need to take a break. after preparing for my exam I was going to sleep but I think between 3 A.M to 3:30 A.M my laptop started saying something like I wanted to play LOLIPOP, come to play ,come to play and I was totally shocked up like I wasn't able to move my hand

, like I was freeze. I just fainted The next morning , I woke up and I saw my mother and father too much tensed. I was fine after the things happened last night , my parents were continously asking me [parents together] What happened you last night ?

[Jessie] I wasn't able to tell them what happened that day, as I was shocked and in depression you can say that..so, I decided to delete the game but whenever I delete it comes over and over again on my laptop. This was really shocking and spooky for me, every night I wasn't able to sleep because of the spooky noise, because of that I became so angry One day I just threw it out of my window, but the next it came back by its own. so, I decided to tell all the things to my parents .They didn't believed me and [parents told] It's nothing sweetie just relax, [Jessie] I tried to convence them but after convencing them for a long time and just told them to sleep or check out my room and then they get to know What happened with me that day.[parents] we are really sorry Jessie We didn't believed you , [Jessie] it's okay mom and dad, but what should we do now ? [Jessie's dad] I think we should go and call a priest. [Jessie's mom] yes, but I think [with a slow moment speaking and watching somewhere else] it is a very wrong idea I think so. [Jessie screamed] and told mom somebody is pulling me help me mom , help me dad [parents scream Jessie]

Mom, please help me it is hurting a lot but suddenly a voice came over I told her I need Jessie If someone called anyone else from this house I will kill Jessie spoke the 'demon' okay fine, we won't call anyone.

Jessie was full day being in a room and but Jessie was smart enough she just called a priest name father Kristoff, he was as the most powerful father in the Churh or in the

Chruch authority. she must send a message and he came over and just stepping of the floor he gets to know there is a bad spirit in Jessie's house. he just started throwing pure or god prays water to everyone in the house and the spirit get to know someone is at home she just wanted to attack the person but she didn't know it was a priest but the father Kristoff was smarter and kept the spirit in a corner captured there and asked her what she want ? [spirit] please let me go, please let me go. [father Kristoff] are you telling or not or you are straight going to hell. [spirit] okay fine , I am Joe , I was just like Jessie but my best friend as the worst he just killed me. [father] why and what happened between you both and why do you need Jessie for it. [spirit Joe] me and my best friend were like the best in our school but suddenly the boy I loved she also started like him and wanted to kill me for getting him. she just killed me on the game and then taken a knife and killed me at the time where Jessie played. [father] so , why do you need Jessie now ? [Joe the spirit] because she is like me and I love to play with her and that's why with that game I can control her and kill my best friend. [the father captured Joe in a bottle and threw her in a ocean and tied a thread on my hand so that she cannot come out] [Jessie] I felt very bad hearing that so I opened the thread and let her free she did her wish done and then went to heaven and I leaved happily and the best part is that whenever I need her help she always come to help me. so, she was THE BEST.......

SHE WAS THE BEST

I just wanted to tell you the next part will be soon and just comment me how was it............

good bye

TWO

THE OLD MAKEN

CH-2- The Old Maken

so here I am going with you again

so, let's just start-

We bought an old house, my boyfriend and me. He's in charge of the "new" construction – converting the kitchen into the master bedroom for instance, while I'm on wallpaper removal duty. The previous owner papered EVERY wall and CEILING! Removing it is brutal but oddly satisfying. The best feeling is getting a long peel, similar to your skin when you're peeling from a sunburn. I don't know about you but I kinda make a game of peeling, on the hunt for the longest piece before it rips . Under a corner section of paper in every room are a person's name and a date. Curiosity got the best of me one night when I Googled one of the names and discovered the person was a missing person, the missing date matching the date under the wallpaper! The next day, I made a list of all the names and dates. Sure enough, each name was for a missing person with dates to match. We notified the police who naturally sent out the crime scene team. I overhead one tech say "yup, it's human." Human? What's human? "Ma'am, where is the material you removed from the walls already? This isn't wallpaper you were removing."

2. 'I hate it when my brother Charlie has to go away by horrorinpureform

I hate it when my brother Charlie has to go away. My parents constantly try to explain to me how sick he is. That I am lucky for having a brain where all the chemicals flow properly to their destinations like undammed rivers. When I complain about how bored I am without a little brother to play with, they try to make me feel bad by pointing out that his boredom likely far surpasses mine, considering his confine to a dark room in an institution. I always beg for them to give him one last chance. Of course, they did at first. Charlie has been back home several times, each shorter in duration than the last. Every time without fail, it all starts again. The neighborhood cats with gouged out eyes showing up in his toy chest, my dad's razors found dropped on the baby slide in the park across the street, mom's vitamins replaced by bits of dishwasher tablets. My parents are hesitant now, using "last chances" sparingly. They say his disorder makes him charming, makes it easy for him to fake normalcy, and trick the doctors who care for him into thinking he is ready for rehabilitation. That I will just have to put up with my boredom if it means staying safe from him. I hate it when Charlie has to go away. It makes me have to pretend to be good until he is back.

3. 'Guardians' by DarkAlliGator

He awoke to the huge, insect-like creatures looming over his bed and screamed his lungs out. They hastily left the room and he stayed up all night, shaking and wondering if it had been a dream. The next morning, there was a tap on the door. Gathering his courage, he opened it to see one of them gently place a plate filled with fried breakfast on the floor, then retreat to a safe distance. Bewildered, he accepted the gift. The creatures chittered excitedly. This happened every day for weeks. At first, he was worried they were fattening him up, but after a particularly greasy breakfast left him clutching his chest from heartburn, they were replaced with fresh fruit. As well as cooking, they poured hot steamy baths for him and even tucked him in when he went to bed. It was bizarre. One night, he awoke to gunshots and screaming. He raced downstairs to find a decapitated burglar being devoured by the insects. He was sickened but disposed of the remains as best he could. He knew they had just been protecting him. One morning the creatures wouldn't let him leave his room. He lay down, confused but trusting as they ushered him back into bed. Whatever their motives, they weren't going to hurt him. Hours later a burning pain spread throughout his body. It felt like his stomach was filled with razor wire. The insects chittered as he spasmed and moaned. It was only when he felt a terrible squirming feeling beneath his skin that he realized the insects hadn't been protecting him. They had been protecting their young.

4. 'Seeing Red (The First Day of School)' by Zenryhao

Everyone loves the first day of school, right? New year, new classes, new friends. It's a day full of potential and hope before all the dreary depressions of reality show up to ruin all the fun. I like the first day of school for a different reason, though. You see, I have a sort of power. When I look at people, I can...sense a sort of aura around them. A colored outline is based on how long that person has to live. Most everyone I meet around my age is surrounded by a solid green hue, which means they have plenty of time left. A fair amount of them has a yellow-orangish tinge to their auras, which tends to mean a car crash or some other tragedy. Anything that takes people "before their time" as they say. The real fun is when the auras venture into the red end of the spectrum, though. Now and again I'll see someone who's a walking stoplight. Those are the ones who get murdered or kill themselves. It's such a rush to see them and knows their time is numbered. With that in mind, I always get to class very early so I can scout out my classmates' fates. The first kid who walked in was radiating red. I chuckled to myself. Too damn bad, bro. But as people kept walking in, they all had the same intense glow. I finally caught a glimpse of my rose-tinted reflection in the window, but I was too stunned to move. Our professor stepped in and locked the door, his aura a sickening shade of green.

5. 'They got the definition wrong' by Liu

It has been said that the definition of insanity is "doing the same thing over and over and expecting different results". I understand the sentiment behind the saying, but it's wrong. I entered the building on a bet. I was strapped for cash and didn't buy into the old legends of the hotel, to begin with, so fifty bucks were more than enough to get me to do it. It was simple. Just reach the top floor, the 45th floor, shine my flashlight from a window. The hotel was old and broken, including the elevator, so that meant hiking up the stairs. So up the stairs, I went. As I reached each platform, I noted the old brass plaques displaying the floor numbers. 15, 16, 17, 18. I felt a little tired as I crept higher, but so far, no ghosts, no cannibals, no demons. Piece of cake. I can't tell you how happy I was as I entered that last stretch of numbers. I joyfully counted them aloud at each platform. 40, 41, 42, 43, 44, 44. I stopped and looked back down the stairs. I must have miscounted, so I continued up. 44. One more flight. 44. And then down ten flights. 44. Fifteen flights. 44. And so it's been for as long as I can remember. So really, insanity isn't doing something repeatedly and expecting different results. It's knowing that the results will never change; that each door leads to the same staircase, to the same number. It's realizing you no longer fall asleep. It's not knowing whether you've been running for days or weeks or years. It's when the sobbing slowly turns into laughter.

6. 'My Daughter Learned to Count' by RealScience87

My daughter woke me around 11:50 last night. My wife and I had picked her up from her friend Sally's birthday party, brought her home, and put her to bed. My wife went into the bedroom to read while I fell asleep watching the Braves game." Daddy," she whispered, tugging my shirt sleeve. "Guess how old I'm going to be next month."I don't know, beauty," I said as I slipped on my glasses. "How old?"She smiled and held up four fingers. It is 7:30 now. My wife and I have been up with her for almost 8 hours. She still refuses to tell us where she got them.

7. 'Timekeeper' by gridster2

He had been given the watch on his tenth birthday. It was an ordinary grey plastic wristwatch in every respect except for the fact that it was counting down. "That is all of the time you have left in the world, son. Use it wisely." And indeed he did. As the watch ticked away, the boy, now a man, lived life to the fullest. He climbed mountains and swam oceans. He talked and laughed and lived and loved. The man was never afraid, for he knew exactly how much time he had left. Eventually, the watch began its final countdown. The old man stood looking over everything he had done, everything he had built. 5. He shook hands with his old business partner, the man who had long been his friend and confidant. 4. His dog came and licked his hand, earning a pat on the head for its companionship. 3. He hugged his son, knowing that he had been a good father. 2. He kissed his wife on the forehead one last time. 1. The old man smiled and closed his eyes.

Then, nothing happened. The watch beeped once and turned off. The man stood standing there, very much alive. You would think that at that moment he would have been overjoyed. Instead, for the first time in his life, the man was scared.

8. 'There's No Reason to be Afraid' by whoever fights the monster

When my sister Betsy and I were kids, our family lived for a while in a charming old farmhouse. We loved exploring its dusty corners and climbing the apple tree in the backyard. But our favorite thing was the ghost. We called her Mother because she seemed so kind and nurturing. Some mornings

Betsy and I would wake up, and on each of our nightstands, we'd find a cup that hadn't been there the night before. Mother had left them there, worried that we'd get thirsty during the night. She just wanted to take care of us. Among the house's original furnishings was an antique wooden chair, which we kept against the back wall of the living room. Whenever we were preoccupied, watching TV or playing a game, Mother would inch that chair forward, across the room, toward us. Sometimes she'd manage to move it to the center of the room. We always felt sad putting it back against the wall. Mother just wanted to be near us. Years later, long after we'd moved out, I found an old newspaper article about the farmhouse's original occupant, a widow. She'd murdered her two children by giving them each a cup of poisoned milk before bed. Then she'd hanged herself. The article included a photo of the farmhouse's living room, with a woman's body hanging from a beam. Beneath her, knocked over, was that old wooden chair placed exactly in the center of the room.

9. 'The Perfect Plan' by Huntfrog

On Monday, I came up with the perfect plan. No one even knew we were friends. On Tuesday, he stole the gun from his dad. On Wednesday, we decided to make our move during the following day's pep rally. On Thursday, while the entire school was in the gym, we waited just outside the doors. I was to use the gun on whoever walked out first. Then he would take the gun and go into the gym blasting. I walked up to Mr. Quinn the guidance counselor and shot him in the face three times. He fell back into the gym, dead. The shots were deafening. We heard screams in the auditorium.No one could see us yet. I handed him the gun and whispered, "your turn." He ran into the gym and started firing. I followed a moment after. He hadn't hit anyone yet. Kids were scrambling and hiding. It was mayhem. I ran up behind him and tackled him. We struggled. I wrenched the gun out of his hands, turned it on him, and killed him. I closed his mouth forever. On Friday, I have anointed a hero. It was indeed the perfect plan.

10. 'Warrior of god' by KMApok

"If God exists, why is there so much evil in the world?" It's a common question, but it is misplaced. All things must have balance. Light and dark. Good and evil. Sound and silence. Without one, the other cannot exist."So if that's true, then God does NOTHING to fight evil?" That might be your follow-up question. Of course, he fights evil. Relentlessly. I am Dartalian, one of His most Holy and Righteous angels. I roam the Earth, disposing of evil wherever I find it. I kill the monsters you don't ever want to know about. I crush them completely so you can sleep at night. You, humans, have no idea how many of you live because of the work I do."But what about Stalin? Hitler? Ted Bundy? Jack the Ripper?"Well, those are the minor ones I had to let live. For balance. The ones I destroy are ....too horrible and vile to survive. What's funny, is while I would wager you never have heard the name Dartalian in any religious texts, I bet you have heard of me. Americans, for example, have their name for me. Sudden Infant Death Syndrome.

11. 'Hell' by MeanPete

There was no pearly gate. The only reason I knew I was in a cave was that I had just passed the entrance. The rock wall rose behind me with no ceiling in sight. I knew this was it, this was what religion talked about, what man feared. I had just entered the gate to hell. I felt the presence of the cave as if it was a living, breathing creature. The stench of rotten flesh overwhelmed me. Then there was the voice, it came from inside and all around."Welcome" Who are you?", I asked, trying to keep my composure."You know", the thing answered. I did know."You are the devil", I stuttered, quickly losing my composure. "Why me? I've lived as good as I could".The silence took over the space as my words died out. It seemed like an hour went by before the response came."What did you expect?"The voice was penetrating but patient."I don't know. I never believed any of this", I uttered, "Is that why I am here?"Silence. I continued: "They say the greatest trick you ever pulled was convincing the world you don't exist" No, the greatest trick I ever pulled was convincing the world that there is an alternative" There is no God?" I shivered. The cave trembled with the words: "I am God."

12. 'The Accident' by miny boy

It was one a.m. and Guy Halverson sat in his dark living room. He hadn't moved for over an hour. The accident earlier that evening kept playing over and over in his mind. The light turned red, but he was in a hurry and accelerated. An orange blur came from his right, and in a split second there was a violent jolt, then the bicyclist rolled across his hood and fell out of sight on the pavement. Horns blared angrily and he panicked, stepping on the gas and screeching away from the chaos into the darkness, shaken and keeping an eye on his rearview mirror until he got home. Why did you run, you idiot? He'd never committed a crime before this and punished himself by imagining years in jail, his career gone, his family gone, his future gone. Why not just go to the police right now? You can afford a lawyer. Then someone tapped on the front door and his world suddenly crumbled away beneath him. They found me. There was nothing he could do but answer it. Running would only make matters worse. His body trembling, he got up, went to the door, and opened it. A police officer stood under the porch light." Mr. Halverson?" asked the grim officer. He let out a defeated sigh. "Yes. Let me —"I am sorry, but I'm afraid I have some bad news. Your son's bike was struck by a hit-and-run driver this evening. He died at the scene. I'm very sorry for your loss."

13. 'Next Time You'll Know Better' by IPostAtMidnight

Have you ever walked into a room and found a vampire? No, not the sexy kind, but a foul creature with bony limbs and ashen skin? The kind that snarls as you enter, like a beast about to pounce? The kind that roots you to the spot with its sunken, hypnotic eyes, rendering you unable to flee as you watch the hideous thing uncoil from the shadows? Has your heart started racing though your legs refuse to? Have you felt time slow as the creature crosses the room in the darkness of a blink? Have you shuddered with fear when it places one clawed hand atop your head and another under your chin so it can tilt you, exposing your neck? Have you squirmed as its rough, dry tongue slides down your cheek, over your jaw, to your throat, in a slithering search that's seeking your artery? Have you felt its hot breath release in a hiss against your skin when it probes your pulse—the flow that leads to your brain? Has its tongue rested there, throbbing slightly as if savoring the moment? Have you then experienced a sinking, sucking blackness as you discover that not all vampires feed on blood—some feed on memories? Well, have you? Maybe not. But let me rephrase the question: Have you ever walked into a room and suddenly forgotten why you came in?

14. 'Hands' by miny boy

The doctor pulled the stethoscope ear tips out and hung the device around his neck."Mr. Weatherby, all of your tests have come back negative and my examination shows nothing abnormal."Adam knew what was coming next. "I'm not crazy, Doctor."I'm sorry, but there is no physical reason why you occasionally lose control of your hands. A psychologist can help..."I don't need therapy. I need answers. They seem to have a life all their own. I can't hold a job. I'm under investigation for assault. I almost killed my neighbor. This can't go on. I'll try anything at this point."After two weeks on a new medication, Adam saw no progress and grew increasingly depressed. He was convinced that despite what the doctors said, it was not a psychological problem. That night, a frustrated and angry Adam sat in a chair and drank bourbon. Drunk and hopeless, he stumbled to the garage and started the table saw, then slowly lowered his wrists toward the screaming blade. Detective Armstrong entered the garage where several uniformed officers stood over the blood-soaked body." So what do we got?" he asked, taking in the blood-splattered scene."This is a weird one, Detective."How so?"Take a look at the body. He chopped off his hands with the table saw and bled to death."Armstrong knelt. "And?"And we can't find his hands anywhere."

15. 'He Stood Against My Window' by sabethook

I don't know why I looked up, but when I did I saw him there. He stood against my window. His forehead rested against the glass, and his eyes were still and light and he smiled a lipstick-red, cartoonish grin. And he just stood there in the window. My wife was upstairs sleeping, my son was in his crib and I couldn't move I froze and watched him looking past me through the glass. Oh, please no. His smile never moved but he put a hand up and slid it down the glass, watching me. With matted hair and yellow skin and face through the window. I couldn't do anything. I just stayed there, frozen, feet still in the bushes I was pruning, looking into my home. He stood against my window.

16. 'Fallers' by dastard82

People started falling from the sky by the close of the decade. They were never clothed, always naked, always a petrifying grin on their faces. It had been just a few at first, but then hundreds and thousands would fall at a time, destroying cars, homes, blocking off highways. Strange discoveries were made upon research; they were human but lacked any blood, intestines, even a heart. No one could explain the hideous grins they had, or even where they came from. It was a woman in Costa Rica who made the latest and most disturbing discovery. She recognized one of the fallen bodies as a long-dead relative, one who died back when she had been a teenager. Then more and more identifications were made. Soon people were picking out their long-dead loved ones amongst the video feeds, cadaver piles, and crematoriums. No one could explain why they were coming back, falling from the sky. Even more distressing, after disposing of the bodies, it wouldn't be long until that same body came plummeting from the sky again. You could not get rid of them, no matter what. People were getting killed by the higher volume of falling bodies, and soon after burial, they too began to fall. My mother was killed when a body landed on her car, crushing her. The next week, the news reported on a body that had gotten lodged in an airplane windshield. I saw my mother's grinning face, the happiest I had ever seen her. They say when hell is full; the dead shall walk the earth. What about heaven?

17. 'The Happiest Day of My Life' by re-clouds

I watched as my soon-to-be father-in-law held his daughter's hand as he walked down the aisle. Tears streamed down his face as the wedding march that played in the background reminded him that, in a few minutes, he would be watching me hold his daughter's hand and slip on her ring. He walked up to the altar and I took hold of her hand, grinning from ear to ear. It was the happiest day of my life. My bride's father got down on his knees and started begging. "Please, I did what you asked. Just please give my daughter back."I glared at him. "Shut up and stop ruining the moment. If you sit back down and enjoy the ceremony, maybe I'll tell you where I've hidden the rest of her body."

18. 'Hidden' by KMApok

"Where are you?!" I scream. Panicked, I run through the abandoned farm. I can't find her. Not in the old house. Not in the barn. I run into the empty field, heart racing. As I scan the area, I run into a mound of dirt and trip, sprawling to the ground. Getting up, it hits me. Abandoned farm. I tripped over freshly tilled earth. Crouching down, I start frantically clawing with my hands. Scooping handfuls of dirt, I hit something hard. Wood."Are you in there?!" I cry, pressing my ear to the wood. I hear muffled cries. I start digging again but realize it's taking too long. Looking around, I see a garden shed. I sprint to it, ripping the door open. I see a shovel, still caked in dirt. Probably the same one that bastard buried her with. I grab it. Running back, I started digging with purpose. Soon the wooden box is exposed. I toss the shovel and rip open the crate. She stares back at me, eyes wide. Bound. Gagged. But alive. I sigh with relief. Thank God. I reach into my bag, pulling out my rag and chloroform. I crouch down, placing it over her face. She struggles, faints. I toss her over my shoulder."Ah, hell!" My brother says as I walk back to the truck with a smirk. "You found her!"Yup. You almost had me though!" I laugh."All right. My turn. Where did you put her?"I gesture to the creek area. "Somewhere over there. Drowning's an issue though." Jerk!" he says, running off. I smile, watching him go. I love adult Hide and Seek.

19. 'My Favorite Support Group' by I Post At Midnight

Look, I'll be the first to admit I'm a complete bastard. I'm also lazy. I'm only here to find the idiot because there's almost always an idiot. This support group is pretty typical. We connected online, decided on a quiet place, and now we're all sitting cross-legged in a circle. Real Kumbaya crap. Jerome takes the lead, pouring everyone a cup of tea as he starts talking."I'm Jerome. You can drink your tea, but only after explaining why you're here. I'll start."Jerome tells us he's never been loved. I can see why—the guy's ugly as sin. He sips his tea while the mousy chick speaks next."Miyu," she says. "My parents."Short and sweet, no blubbering. Gotta admire Miyu. She's probably not the idiot. Next to talk are a legless veteran, a broke businessman, a needle-tracked junkie, and a diseased old crone. Then it's my turn."I'm an ass. Everyone hates me."I take a loud, annoying slurp of oolong as the fat kid with a black eye goes next, telling his boring fat-kid sob story. Afterward, we're all sitting quietly when Jerome keels over. Then Miyu's eyes roll back and she slumps forward. Only the fat kid reacts."What's happening?" he whines. "I thought this was a suicide support group!"Found the idiot."It is," I say, spitting out my mouthful of tea. "They support it. No one wants to die alone, kid."Oh, how ghost-white he turns, looking into his cup! I love it! These suicide meetups are a sadist's dream, and I never have to lift a finger. Told you I'm a lazy bastard.

20. 'ylim3' by IPostAtMidnight

Little Emily vanished last year. Now they're pouring new sidewalks in my neighborhood, and I've found her name in the wet cement, written in remembrance. But it was written in reverse. And from below.

21. 'The Eyes are Watching Me' by recluse

I bought a new house in the small town of Winthrop. The house was cheap, but the most important part was that I needed to get away from the city. A few months ago, I had a run-in with a stalker. While I had managed to get him arrested, I couldn't shake the feeling of eyes just constantly watching me. I felt like there were eyes everywhere, at home and on the street, so I decided to move out into the country to somewhere with fewer people, just for peace of mind. The house itself was big and somewhat old, but otherwise very welcoming. The agent who introduced me to the house had been required to mention that a serial killer had lived here in the past, which was why the house was so cheap. However, he, and later, my next-door neighbor Sarah, both told me to pay the thought no mind. Four other owners had lived in the house since then, and all of them were very happy with it. I loved the house. Its interior furnishings were beautiful and very comfortable. The people of Winthrop were friendly, often bringing over freshly baked pastries or inviting me over for dinner. "Get-togethers," they said, "were the key to making sure everyone who lived in Winthrop loved it there."Yet after a week, I stopped "loving it." The feeling of someone watching returned, worse than before. I tried to ignore it, but soon I started losing sleep. Giant bags grew under my eyes and I began yawning almost as much as I breathed. Sarah was kind enough to let me stay in her house for a few nights. It was during this time that I heard the legend of Forrest Carter, the serial killer who had lived in my house. While no one knows his exact kill count, Carter, also known as the Winthrop Peacock, was a man with an extremely severe case of narcissism. Legends say that he couldn't fall asleep if he didn't feel like he was being watched. He was finally arrested for putting up a scarecrow to watch him during the night. Only it wasn't a scarecrow. Carter had murdered a 17-year-old girl, just so her corpse could stare at him. The story gave me shivers, and after I went home, I felt like there were hundreds of pairs of eyes just watching me no matter how I turned. Today, however, was the first day that I acted out. I was cooking breakfast when I felt the eyes. Instinctively, out of fear, I threw my kitchen knife, which lodged itself into the wall. As I pulled it out, I found myself staring at a pair of eyes, pickling in formaldehyde. I've been watching the police peel away the drywall of my house for hours now. So far, they've found

142 pairs of eyes in little glass jars. The scariest thing is, everyone was staring at me.

22. 'The twist at the end' - ai1267

Cradling my four-year-old daughter in my arms, all I could do was listen as the screaming outside the house got louder and louder, interspersed with sounds of violence and horrible, horrible wet thuds and the unmistakable echo of muscle and sinew resisting the force that was slowly tearing them apart. It started just three days ago. Something happened, out there in the world, and before we even get news of what's going on, seemingly half of the world is gone. Police and military were unable to stop it, providing such a short frame of resistance it's hard to know whether it was real or just a fluke. There was no centralized target, no way to use our most powerful weapons, not without incinerating ourselves in the process. They poured forth across the world, from wherever it was that it started. I hear banging on the door downstairs, and the screams of people being slaughtered, unable to mount a proper resistance against such a force. It doesn't take long before the pounding gives way to splintering and the sound of shattering wood. They're in the house.No more than a moment or two passes before the door to the bedroom start shuddering. The things I piled against it are holding, for now, but I know, realistically, that they're going to manage to come through. I keep rocking my little girl, humming a lullaby in her ear to calm her as she cries. The pounding grows in force and volume, the frame starting to crack. I put my little girl on my lap, her back to my chest, and I stroke her head with both hands, from the top of her scalp, down across her ears, just as I've done ever since she was a baby.

Just the way she loves it. The effect is instantaneous. Her desperate crying calms to a series of sobs and hiccoughs, her small body shuddering against mine in fear. I keep humming to her, soothing her hair, acting for all the world as if nothing is out of place, not a single thing amiss. Agonizingly slowly, in a reverse cadence of the sound of splintering wood, she calms down. I can feel it when she stops tensing, as I keep stroking her down the sides of her head. A final hiccough of a sob and she falls quiet, her body relaxed. She doesn't even have time to realize what's happening as I twist her neck with a violent jerk, accompanied by a dry snap of a sound. She's dead before she can even slump down into my lap. The door is giving way, the furniture is pushed back. I may be torn limb from limb while I scream, but at least my baby angel's safe from harm.

23. 'Crying isn't going to help' by HonestRage

I pointed the gun at the sick bastard who killed my wife. He sobbed as he feared for what was to come. I pulled the trigger. If only he spoke and tried to reason with me then maybe he could've lived. But that was not going to happen. After all, he was born just a few minutes ago.

24. 'Return of the Messiah' by Huntfrog

In the year 2026, the Messiah came back down to Earth. She performed miracles and cured the sick. There was no doubt as to her authenticity. She appeared to all nations at once. All believed. All worshipped her.

Sometime later, after this period of our history known as the Age of Peace, She dropped a bombshell on us. She warned us that Heaven was almost full. Nobody had gone to Hell during this Age. There were a fixed amount of spots left. Paradise would be closed to all who died after the Gates close.

That is when the Mass Suicides began. Taking your own life, She had told us, was not a sin if you died a pious man. The race was on!

She looked on and was pleased. She returned to her home, to her throne of fire and flames, and greeted all with a nod of her wicked horns.

25. 'The Enemy' by AG_plus

I flung myself through the door and vaulted the toppled, long-dead refrigerator that served as an ineffective barricade in front of me. My legs propelled me through the room and into the small hallway on the other side. I couldn't stop eating the expired contents of the fridge, appealing to me despite their stench after several days without food. The shrieks of pain and cries for mercy around me spurred my body onward and filled me with unexpected energy despite my hunger. We were at war. I came to a halt in front of a small bathroom. A noise. Something behind the shower curtain. My fear heightened and images of the enemy flooded my mind. Merciless beasts wearing human skin, devouring indiscriminately, accepting no pleas, and respecting no argument. Zombies. It had begun as we expected, with a virus. The original infected was almost a cliché. There was no humanity left in them. Just mindless rage, twisted bodies, and some primal urge to consume others. Our generation had prepared, with almost obsessive focus, for this monster. The first wave was eradicated with almost laughable ease. We were not prepared for adaptation. We were not prepared for the creature we bred by destroying the instantly recognizable zombie. A creature with more tact. Most of the first zombies were killed at close range, you understand, since longer-range attacks were less likely to be fatal. We had trained ourselves, even before the outbreak, to equate "infection" with "death" when it came to zombies. A person "died" when their eyes clouded over and they started biting, not when you put a bullet in their head. The new strain of the virus still controlled the body, yes, but it left other faculties to the host. Maybe you could pull the trigger on a hopelessly crazed caricature of your best friend, your spouse, your child. But what if there was still a soul behind those eyes? If even as they attacked, they sobbed and screamed in their voice? All the virus needed was a moment's hesitation. I bet you'd hesitate. I did. This is why now I could only watch as my arm wrenched back the shower curtain and my hands reached for the cowering child. Why I could only beg for forgiveness before the virus used my mouth to tear ragged, bloody chunks from his body. Why I couldn't even vomit as my hunger dissipated with the now sickeningly familiar taste of human flesh. We were at war. And I am the enemy.

26. 'So I lost my phone...' by Lynxx

Last night a friend rushed me out of the house to catch the opening act at a local bar's music night. After a few drinks, I realized my phone wasn't in my pocket. I checked the table we were sitting at, the bar, the bathrooms, and after no luck, I used my friend's phone to call mine. After two rings someone answered, gave out a low raspy

giggle, and hung up. They didn't answer again. I eventually gave it up as a lost cause and headed home. I found my phone laying on my nightstand, right where I left it.

27. 'The Brave Ones' by scary-Maxx

Here they come again, the brave ones. Another Halloween night and the kids are back, here to prove their fearlessness. The old house's floorboards creak beneath their sneakers. Only half an hour until midnight, so I have to work fast. I start with their flashlight, blowing lightly against it so that it flickers, but this inspires little more than a nervous giggle. Fifteen minutes until midnight. Time to take things up a notch. I hover up to the ceiling, and will my body into flesh. My every nerve is on fire, but they've given me no choice. I force drops of blood to trickle out my nose, but the boys below don't notice. I knock against the ceiling, but they won't even look up." I thought this place was supposed to be haunted," says the leader. "What a joke."Five minutes until midnight. I'm running out of time. With the last of my strength, I scream— so loud that they finally turn to look up at me. I like to think I put on a good show: I sway on an invisible noose, and the blood flows freely from my nostrils now. A couple of drops hit a skinny one with a crew cut. The boys scream and run into the night, just in time. Below me, I hear the Thing turn, its disappointment palpable. For now, it sleeps. But one day, I will fail. The boys will be too brave, and I won't scare them out in time. One day they will wake it.

28. 'Nap in the car' by _b_o_o_

Mommy always leaves me and daddy home on Saturday nights, and I and daddy always go get ice cream in the car after dinner. I have to sit in the back seat until I'm a big boy. I go in the kitchen to see what daddy is cooking for dinner after my Barney movie is over, but he's not in there this time. I saw a note on the counter that said mommy and uncle James were going somewhere together. I'm not sure, I don't read that well. I go find daddy in the garage. I shut the door behind me like I'm supposed to. Daddy is in the car and he already has the car turned on. We must not be eating dinner tonight, only ice cream. I get in the backseat behind daddy since I'm not a big boy yet. Daddy doesn't say anything when I said hello to him. Maybe he can't hear me over the loud car. I think I'll take a nap on the way to ice cream. I feel kinda sleepy.

29. 'What they don't tell you about the dead' by Crimson

I don't want to sound mean, but the dead are pretty clueless. I've always seen them. When I was younger everyone thought I was just talking to imaginary friends. After a couple of years, when I overheard my parents talk about calling a psychologist, I realized what I was talking to. See, ghosts don't tend to realize they're dead, and they don't look like in the movies, they look just like us. I'm pretty smart for a 13-year-old, so I started noticing certain patterns to tell them apart from the living. They could be a bit distant from living people, or you'd see them try to talk to people who wouldn't even notice them. Some of them could tell I was different, that I noticed them. Like this guy, I saw after school yesterday. I'm a big boy now, see, I don't need my parents to pick me up, home is just a short walk away. He was standing away from the other parents, didn't talk to them, just stared at me, that's how I knew he was one of the ghosts. I went over, told him I knew what he was, and asked how I could help him. I don't remember much after that, I think because of what happened this morning. Downstairs, my parents were crying. I tried talking to them but they ignored me. They must have died last night somehow, sometimes the new ghosts wouldn't talk to me. Some police officers and reporters just arrived, they won't talk to me either, just my parents. It's weird, I've never seen so many ghosts together before. Why won't anyone talk to me?

30. 'A Message from your Personal Demons' by MRGram

Hello, my dear. You do not know who I am, but I know you. I am one of the three demons that were assigned to you at birth. You see, some people in this world are destined for greatness, destined to live happy, fulfilling lives. You, I am afraid, are not one of those people, and it is our job to make sure of that. Who are we? Oh yes, of course, how rude of me. Allow me to introduce us: Shame is my younger brother, the demon on your left shoulder. Shame tells you that you're a freak; that those thoughts you have are not normal; that you will never fit in. Shame whispered into your ear when your mother found you playing with yourself as a child. Shame is the one who makes you hate yourself. Fear sits on your right shoulder. He is my older brother, as old as life itself. Fear fills every dark corner with monsters, turns every stranger on a dark street into a murderer. Fear stops you from telling your crush how you feel. He tells you it is better not to try than let people see you fail. Fear makes you build your prison. Who am I, then? I am the worst of your demons, but you see me as a friend. You turn to me when you have nothing else because I live in your heart. I am the one who forces you to endure. The one who prolongs your torment.Sincerely, Hope.

9 798886 064605

Printed by Libri Plureos GmbH in Hamburg,
Germany